HENRY AND AMY

(right-way-round and upside down)

For
Brother Dave
(Sandy &
Imogen)
and
Sister Mel
(Tyrone)

Miranda and
Charlotte,
(Mandy
& Pam)

Mark
and Liz,
(Hannah)

Trish
and Tani

First published in Australia by Scholastic Australia Pty. Limited; published in the United States of America in 1999 by Walker Publishing Company, Inc.

Library of Congress Cataloging-in-Publication Data
King, Stephen Michael.
Henry and Amy (right-way-round and upside down)/Stephen Michael King.
p.   cm.
Summary: Even though they are very different, Henry and Amy are good friends.
ISBN 0-8027-8686-3 (hardcover). —ISBN 0-8027-8687-1 (reinforced)
[1. Friendship—Fiction. 2. Individuality—Fiction.] I. Title.
PZ7.K58915He 1999
[E]—dc21   98-33281
                                                                                CIP
                                                                                AC

Printed in Hong Kong
10 9 8 7 6 5 4 3 2 1

HENRY AND AMY
(right-way-round and upside down)

Stephen Michael King

WALKER AND COMPANY
NEW YORK

Every time Henry tried
to draw a straight line . . .

it

turned

out

wiggly.

When everyone around him looked up . . .

Henry
looked
down.

If he thought it was going
to be a beautiful sunny day . . .

it would rain.

Splish

Splash

Sploosh

arly one morning when Henry
was out walking backward,
trying very hard to walk forward,

he bumped into Amy.

Amy could do everything right.

She *never* tied her shoelaces together

or buttered the wrong side of her toast.

She always remembered her umbrella

and could even write her name.

Henry thought everything Amy did was amazing.

So Amy showed him his **right** from his **left**,

his **front** from his **back,**

and that the sky was up
and the ground was down.

One day they decided
to build a treehouse.

Amy worked on a plan so that
it would sit in the tree just right.

Henry added lots of squiggly wiggly
bits that made them both giggle.

Deep down, Amy
wished everything she
did wasn't so perfect.

So Henry found
her a coat and a hat
that didn't match.

Then he taught Amy
back-to-front

and
topsy-turvy.

They rolled down a hill sideways . . .

and together they
learned how to fly.

Henry and Amy are the
very, very best of friends . . .

right-way-round

and upside down.